KU-067-982

Wolf Hill

Million-Dollar Egg

Roderick Hunt

Illustrated by Alex Brychta

Oxford University Press

Oxford University Press, Great Clarendon Street, Oxford, OX2 6DP

Oxford   New York
Athens   Auckland   Bangkok   Bogota   Buenos Aires   Calcutta
Cape Town   Chennai   Dar es Salaam   Delhi   Florence   Hong Kong
Istanbul   Karachi   Kuala Lumpur   Madrid   Melbourne   Mexico City
Mumbai   Nairobi   Paris   São Paulo   Singapore   Taipei   Tokyo
Toronto   Warsaw

and associated companies in
Berlin   Ibadan

Oxford is a trade mark of Oxford University Press

© text Roderick Hunt 1998
© illustrations Alex Brychta
First Published 1998

ISBN 019 918666 9

Printed in Hong Kong

Chapter 1

How much is an egg worth? Not much. Not unless it's special.

Chris's mum was cooking.

'I need some eggs,' she said.

Chris and his brother Steve were watching television. Their mum came in from the kitchen. She had flour on her hands. She turned off the television.

'Oh Mum!' said Steve. 'We were watching that. Can't we go later?'

'Go and get them now,' she said. 'I need them quickly.'

'How much are a dozen eggs?' asked Chris.

'Not much,' said his mum. She gave him some coins from her purse.

4

'I want fresh eggs,' she said. 'Don't go to the shop. Get them from Archie.'

Archie's eggs were special. They were fresh. Sometimes they were still warm when you bought them.

One of Archie's eggs was very special. It was the million-dollar egg.

Chapter 2

Everyone liked Archie. His shop was on Wolf Hill Road. It was called The Outpost. Archie sold eggs, honey, apples and potatoes. Every winter he sold Christmas trees.

Years ago, Archie had put up a sign. It was made out of big wooden letters. It said 'The Outpost - Free Range Eggs'. Most of the letters had fallen off now. Only a few were left. The sign made everyone laugh.

Archie's place was like a little farm. He kept chickens and geese. He had two goats and a donkey called Poppy.

Chris and Steve liked going to Archie's. They set off to get the eggs.

At the same time, a big car drove into The Outpost. The car meant trouble for Archie.

Chapter 3

Chris and Steve went to Archie's shop. The shop was really just an old shed. It was locked. A sign said:

'Closed. Back in 10 minutes'

A black car was parked near the shed. It had tinted windows. You couldn't see who was inside it.

'Smart car!' said Steve.

Cars often stopped at Archie's.
People pulled in to buy things.

The black car was different.
Nobody got out.

'Let's find Archie,' said Steve. Chris
and Steve turned to go. As they went,
Chris looked back at the black car.

He saw the window slide down.

Then he saw a hand holding a camera. Someone in the car was taking photographs.

Archie's place was a mess. It was just old sheds and wooden shacks. Why would anyone take photographs of Archie's place?

Chapter 4

Archie was feeding the hens. He was throwing corn on the ground.

The hens ran up squawking and flapping. They pecked up the corn.

'Silly birds,' said Archie.

'Hello, Archie. A dozen eggs, please,' said Steve.

Archie's donkey looked over the
fence. She made a noise like a rusty
trumpet.

'Can I give her a carrot?' asked
Chris.

Archie had a bucket full of old
cabbage leaves. 'Give her one of
these,' he said.

Chris held out a leaf. 'Here you are,
Poppy,' he said. Poppy took it in her
yellow teeth.

Archie looked back down the path.
'That's funny,' he said.

Two people were looking at
Archie's place – a man and a woman.
The woman had a camera.

'What are they doing?' asked
Archie.

Chapter 5

Who were those people? They hadn't come to buy eggs. They wanted a lot more than that. They wanted Archie's place.

That's why they were taking photographs.

They didn't want the old sheds and chicken coops. They didn't want Archie's old cottage. They wanted the land.

The Outpost was in the middle of a busy town. The land was very valuable. It was a good place to build a factory.

16

'The old man will have to go,' said the woman with the camera.

'Will you tell him, then?' said the man.

The woman looked at Chris and Steve. 'Wait until those kids have gone,' she said. 'Then you can tell him.'

Chapter 6

The next day, Archie went to Wolf Hill School. Mr Saffrey was in his office. Archie knocked at the door.

'Hello, Archie,' said Mr Saffrey. 'What can I do for you?'

Archie took something out of a bag. It was a musical box.

'I want the school to have this,' he said.

Mr Saffrey looked at the box. 'It's beautiful,' he said.

Archie opened the lid. The musical box played a tune.

'It plays six tunes,' said Archie. 'It's very old. Not many children have seen a musical box like this.'

'But it must be valuable,' said Mr Saffrey. 'You shouldn't give it away.'

Archie looked sad. 'I'm clearing stuff out,' he said. 'I've got to move. Some people want to buy The Outpost. It doesn't belong to me. It's not my land, you see.'

'That's terrible,' said Mr Saffrey.
'Can't you stop them?'

'I'd buy the land myself but I can't afford it,' said Archie. 'I'd need to be a millionaire!'

Chapter 7

There was a story about Archie in the newspaper. Chris's mum read it out. It said 'End of The Outpost.' There was a photograph of Archie with Poppy.

'No more fresh eggs from Archie,' said Chris's mum. 'He's being turned out. They want to build a factory.'

Chris was angry.

'It's not fair,' he said. 'What will happen to Archie's animals?'

'It's not just that,' said Steve. 'Who wants a factory? It's too near the school.'

'I feel sorry for Archie,' said their
mum. 'He's been there for years. He
was there when I was a girl.'

'Can't we stop them?' said Chris.

'How?' said Steve.

24

'I don't know,' said Chris. 'There must be something we can do.'

'I don't think there is,' said Chris's mum.

There was something. And it was Chris who did it.

Chapter 8

Mr Saffrey was angry. 'They can't turn Archie out,' he said. 'And we don't want a factory. It's too near the school.'

He got in the school mini-bus and drove to The Outpost.

Archie was outside his shop. He was painting a sign. It said, 'Sale – everything must go.'

'I can sell all my junk,' said Archie, 'but I what can I do with my animals?'

'Nobody wants you to go,' said Mr Saffrey. 'We don't want a factory here. We've got to stop it.'

'What can we do?' said Archie.

'We could hold a protest,' said Mr Saffrey.

Archie looked surprised. 'A protest?' he said. 'Who would come to a protest?'

'Leave it to me,' said Mr Saffrey.

Chapter 9

The protest was held on Saturday. Lots of children from Wolf Hill School came with their families.

Chris and Steve were there. Chris's mum had made a banner. It said, 'No factory here.'

The protest started at the Town Hall. Mr Saffrey stood on the steps.

Chris was excited. All of his friends were there. Loz and her Nan were there. So were Kat and Arjo.

The protest march began. Chris walked with Andy. Andy's mum had made a banner, too.

'Thank you for coming,' shouted Mr Saffrey. 'We are going to march to The Outpost. Remember. This is a peaceful protest. We want no trouble.'

Mr Saffrey didn't know it, but there was trouble ahead.

Chapter 10

It took a long time to get to The Outpost. The marchers turned into Archie's. Then they stopped.

A crowd of people blocked the way. A large truck was parked by Archie's shop. There was a big banner on it. It said, 'A factory means jobs.'

A woman stood on the truck. She had a loud hailer. 'Don't stop progress! A factory will bring jobs. Jobs bring money.'

The people began to cheer.

Archie ran up to Mr Saffrey. He looked pale. 'I couldn't stop them,' he said. 'They just turned up.'

Some of the marchers started shouting.

'Please!' called Mr Saffrey. 'No trouble!'

Chris looked at the woman on the
truck. He spoke to Archie. 'I've seen
her before,' he said. 'She's the woman
who had the camera.'

'You're right!' said Archie. 'Well
done, Chris! I have an idea. Get
some of your friends. Go down to the
hens.'

Chapter 11

Chris got his friends. Archie was already with the hens.

'Find as many eggs as you can,' said Archie. 'Look everywhere. Then bring them up to the shop.'

The children began looking for the eggs. They were hard to find.

'Why does he want eggs?' asked
Kat.

'Can't you guess?' said Andy. 'To
throw at those people!'

'We need to look in all the hen
houses,' said Chris. 'I'll try in this
one.'

Chris crawled inside. It smelt
terrible. A hen was sitting on a ledge.
It clucked and flapped down. It had
been sitting on an egg.

Chris reached up for the egg.
Above him he saw a woman in blue.
She was holding a baby.

'Oh wow!' he said.

Chapter 12

Archie handed out the eggs. He shouted at the people round the lorry. 'We know who you are! You're getting paid to be here!'

He pointed to the woman on the truck. 'She's paying you.'

'What if she is?' one of the people shouted.

Archie threw the first egg. It hit the
woman on the side of the head. The
yellow yolk ran down her neck.

'Great shot!' shouted Loz's Nan.

Eggs began to fly towards the truck.
The people tried to duck. Some of
them ran away.

The battle with the eggs didn't last long. The woman got in the truck. An egg went 'splat' on the windscreen. The truck drove away. The protesters cheered.

Chris tugged Mr Saffrey's jacket.

'I've found something,' he said.

Chapter 13

Some men took off the roof of the hen house.

'Be careful!' one of them said. 'Oh dear! Look at all these nails!'

At last the roof came apart. Under one half was a dusty old painting.

The man looked at it carefully.
'Beautiful!' he said. 'It's four
hundred years old. It's worth a
fortune.'

Everyone gasped.

'It was when I found that egg,' said Chris. 'I looked up, and there was the picture.'

'To think I used it to make a hen house,' said Archie. 'I think I'm going to faint!'

'That egg wasn't real,' said Chris. 'It was made of china.'

'Yes,' said Archie. 'I put it there. I've got lots of them. They help hens to lay eggs.'

'This one's special,' said Chris. 'It helped me find the painting. May I keep it?'

Chapter 14

Archie's painting was worth a
fortune. It was sold in America.

A museum paid a million dollars
for it.

Archie bought The Outpost.

'I can afford to retire now,' said Archie. 'I going to make The Outpost into a park. I want children to enjoy it.'

'That's great,' said Chris. 'Thanks, Archie!'

'Thank you, Chris,' said Archie. 'It was you who found the million-dollar egg!'